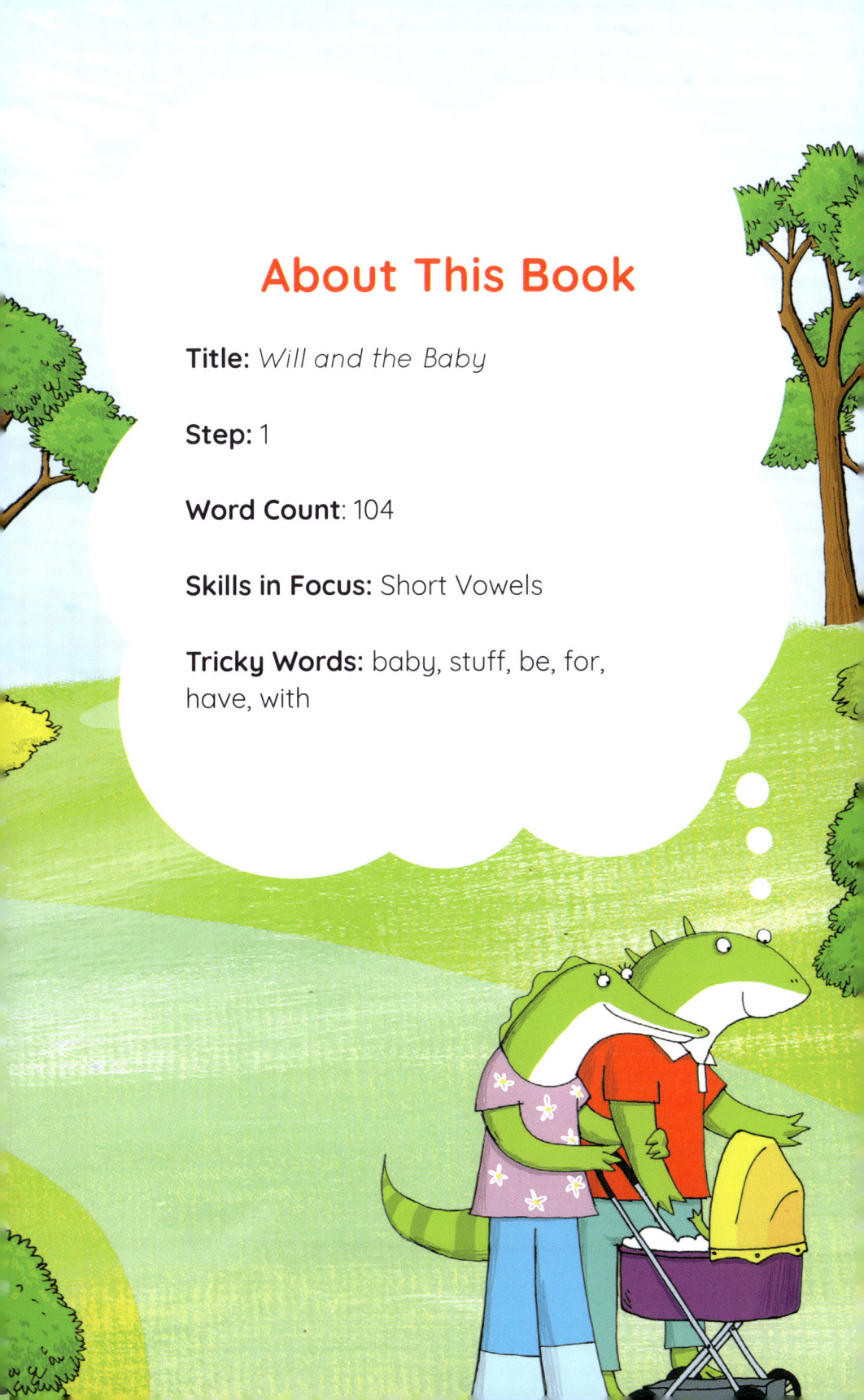

About This Book

Title: *Will and the Baby*

Step: 1

Word Count: 104

Skills in Focus: Short Vowels

Tricky Words: baby, stuff, be, for, have, with

Ideas for Using this Book

Before Reading:
- **Comprehension:** Look at the title and cover image together. Have the students welcomed a new baby or other members to the family? What might that be like? Ask the reader to make a prediction.
- **Accuracy:** Practice the tricky words listed on Page 1.
- **Phonemic Awareness:** Have readers listen as you segment the sounds in the word *Will* (w-i-l). What word is it? What short vowel sound do you hear? Repeat with other short vowel story words: *fun*, *can*, and *mom*.

During Reading:
- Have the reader point under each word as they read it.
- **Decoding:** If stuck on a word, help readers say each sound and blend it together smoothly.
- **Comprehension:** Invite students to add to or change their prediction from before reading.

After Reading:
Discuss the book. Some ideas for questions:
- How does Will feel about the baby's upcoming arrival? How do you know?
- What do you think Will read about in his book, *The Big Kid and the Baby*?
- Why does Will perform big kid activities with Mom and Dad before the baby's arrival?

Will and the Baby

Text by
Leanna Koch

Educational Content by
Kristen Cowen

Illustrated by
Andrew Rowland

PICTURE WINDOW BOOKS
a capstone imprint

This is Mom, Dad, and Will.
Mom will have a baby.

Will can get stuff for the baby.

Dad has fun with Will.

Mom has fun with Will.

"I am a big kid!" Will tells Dad.

Dad nods. "Yes, Will is a big kid."

"I can have fun in the sun!"
Will tells Mom.

Mom sips and nods.
"Yes, this is fun!"

Will will be the baby's big kid pal.
It will be fun.

Will runs to hug the baby.

"This will be fun!" Will tells the baby.
"Yes!" Mom and Dad nod.

More Ideas:

Phonemic Awareness Activity

Practicing Short Vowels:
Tell the students to listen as you stretch the sounds of a story word. Model using a rubber band (or any other stretchy object) as you stretch the word, saying each sound slowly. The students will say the word. Repeat and have the students say the sounds slowly as you stretch the rubber band. Repeat the word. What is the short vowel sound?

- g-e-t
- f-u-n
- h-o-p
- p-a-l
- w-i-th

Extended Learning Activity

Main Events:
Will did many things to have fun while preparing for the baby's arrival. Have readers draw three events from the story that show Will's actions.

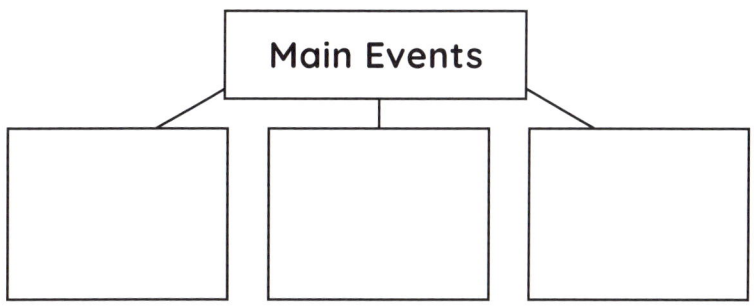

Published by Picture Window Books,
an imprint of Capstone
1710 Roe Crest Drive,
North Mankato, Minnesota 56003
capstonepub.com

Will and the Baby was originally published as
Little Lizard's New Baby, copyright 2011 by Stone Arch Books.

Copyright © 2024 by Capstone.
All rights reserved. No part of this publication may be reproduced
in whole or in part, or stored in a retrieval system, or transmitted in
any form or by any means, electronic, mechanical, photocopying,
recording, or otherwise, without written permission of the publisher.

Library of Congress Cataloging-in-Publication Data is available
on the Library of Congress website.

ISBN: 9780756595944 (hardback)
ISBN: 9781484697917 (paperback)
ISBN: 9781484698112 (eBook PDF)

Printed and bound in the USA. 5757